JACKASS

SHORT STORY COLLECTION

RICK GLAZE

ScreenShot Publishers
Nashville, TN
Ricksbooks@rickglaze.com

These stories are works of fiction. Any names, characters, companies, organizations, places, events, locales, and incidents are either used in a fictitious manner or are fictional. Any resemblance to actual persons, living or dead, actual companies or organizations, or actual events is purely coincidental.

ScreenShot Publishers™

Cover Design: Go Logo Now
ISBN: 978-1-7372951-9-8 Paperback
ISBN: 978-1-7372951-8-1 Ebook

Also by Rick Glaze

Novels:

The Purple River
Spanish Pieces of Eight
Eight Pieces of Eight
Ralph & Murray

Silicon Cowboy (music CD)
Anegada Caribbean Breeze (music CD)

Visit Rick's website and join his **Premium Reader Club** for updates on the Islands, Sailing Adventures and new stories for our subscribers.

www.RickGlaze.com

Contents

PREFACE

Short stories are a unique writing medium and a treat for a novelist and songwriter. Like songwriting, a short story is a way to deliver a punch with a single idea or "hook" as the Nashville cats call it.

Jackass came from my second trip ascending from the bottom to the top of the Grand Canyon. Hiking the Bright Angel Trail, I saw a lush valley and fertile streams running down to the Colorado River, but the Kaibab Trail follows a dry lifeless but breathlessly austere path that is like no other. I was writing my first novel, *The Purple River*, at the time and was compelled to take a break from it to allow this tale to unfold.

It's a Date is a fun dialogue the vibe of which I heard over and over again in thirty-five years living in Silicon Valley.

Trust me, that's really the way it is.

Balls on a Brass Monkey, The Seatmate is my lighthearted take on coping with the monotonous drone of political correctness. Lake Tahoe skiing is an enticing backdrop for this humorous yarn.

The Blast was written during a fascination with psychic topics like telekinesis as well as a preponderance of tragic events from worldwide terrorism. The story takes a light approach with a hint of the paranormal.

Two More Pieces of Pie was written after a long weekend wine tasting with my poker buddies. Yes, we found that Roadhouse near Paso Robles, and yes when the band finished, we jumped up on stage and rocked the house with our eclectic folk/jazz blend of jamming. And yes, there was a granddaughter who jumped on stage to help out between waitress duties. *You can't make this stuff up!* These are fun stories for your amusement!

JACKASS

"Get up now...go on...get going you nice mule," Bob cajoled his mount as he lightly nudged the under belly of the animal with his heels. His toes stayed snug in the stirrups.

Turning his neck, he peered over his right shoulder into the deepest part of the gorge. This ancient mud, more than 1.8 billion years old, was heated and compressed to form Vishnu Schist, the densest rock on the planet.

"I don't know what's wrong with this stupid mule. He just stopped. Maybe he's afraid of falling off the trail. God knows I am. It's only about two thousand feet to that eighty-ton rock that will stop a person...and break his neck, not to mention every other bone in his body. Maybe he's thirsty? You think he'll drink out of this plastic water bottle? Get this trusty stead moving. Hi-ho Silver and all that stuff."

Bob's friend dismounted, walked back a few steps to face the immovable mule. He took the bridle that wrapped around the animal's nose, stood back at arm's length and jerked the leather strap. The mule didn't look up. He didn't move his head. He didn't move a single leg. He didn't move anything. He just stood his ground.

"Good morning. Okay to pass by?" a hiker asked politely. The narrow path as well as the large farm animal planted right in the middle of the trail intimidated the unassuming mountaineer.

"Yeah, okay by me," Bob replied. "I don't think this mule is going to race you up the mountain."

"Where did you get the mules?" the hiker asked.

"Phantom Ranch at the bottom. Started about 6:30 this morning."

"Just you two?" the hiker continued.

"The wrangler went ahead with a larger group of tourists, all wearing new white tennis shoes, but thanks for asking," Bob said. "I was just starting to feel like Wild Bill Hickock when this trusty mount stopped dead in its tracks."

Bob's friend looked up in silence and stared at him.

"Okay, okay, I'm getting off Trigger and we can both pull," Bob grunted.

Bob dismounted, straightened his bowed legs and stepped to the front of the mule. They both heaved on the bridle. The mule didn't budge.

"Let's get a coordinated effort here. On the count of three, pull. One, two, three."

Bob bent his elbow slightly, planted his waffle-soled-buckle-up hiking sandals on the sandy rock path, leaned back and they both tugged on the leather straps again. Bob held his breath for more strength and when he couldn't hold it any more, he exhaled, let go of the straps and gasped for a mouth full of the fresh morning canyon air. The mule didn't move.

"Okay, you get in back and push and I'll pull. That way we'll let this beast know we're serious. Just put your shoulder into his backside," Bob exclaimed.

His friend stepped carefully around the mule on the outside of the narrow path. He walked past the beast to a small, wide spot created by the path switching direction as it wound up the hill. Both edges of this switchback were lined with flat rocks embedded about four inches into the soil and covered with a gritty-dust patina. Without regard for his waiting companion, Bob sat on one of the rocks, slowly unscrewed the top of his plastic bottle and took a long drink of the sunbaked water. He could see all the way to the north rim of the Grand Canyon. The vertical cliffs of the red wall limestone glistened orange in the morning sun. The eight-thousand-foot elevation of the rim itself, hid the high desert plain beyond it.

"We're not waiting for a bus here, let's go," Bob shouted to his friend.

Both took their positions and on the usual count they pulled and pushed over and over. They both broke into a sweat as a cool breeze swept down from higher up the path and blew a shower of sand and dust on the two travelers and their saddled beasts. The mule still didn't move.

"Goddamn it! Move, you fucking jackass!" Bob shouted.

"Actually, his father was a jackass, although I prefer to call him a donkey, and his mother was a horse. He is a mule," a hiker said to Bob.

The late middle-aged woman was passing by on the outside of the path just as Bob and his friend collapsed on the sandy path in exhaustion. Her face was thin and she looked trim with fitted shorts and designer camping socks neatly folded over mildly broken in canvass hiking boots. Her salt and pepper hair hung down to the middle of her neck.

"Yes, I know he is a mule, I was talking to you, my dear lady!" Bob retorted.

The hiker's smile faded and she accelerated her pace up the mountain without another word. Bob stared at the mule. The mule stared back. Bob suddenly charged, waving his arms and screaming, but stopped short of the animal, who looked down at the path in front of him but didn't move.

The path became a busy thoroughfare as the morning progressed. Some would say 'hi,' others would just look at the mule and Bob and do their best to squeeze along the constricted path and continue down to the bottom of the gorge or up to the rim. There were no clouds and the cobalt blue sky was matched in awesome beauty by fifteen miles of rugged peaks from rim to rim, schist to shale. A thirty-something man, balding with a scruffy beard stopped, popped off the waist strap of his frame pack and hoisted his load of camping gear off his shoulders onto the ground. He leaned the tightly packed bundle against a wall of rock.

"Mule won't move?" he asked.

Bob rolled his eyes but said nothing.

His friend nodded to the camper, "That's right, mule won't move."

"Want a granola bar?" the camper offered.

"No thanks," Bob said.

Bob's friend looked up and held out his hand. The camper reached into his shirt pocket, pulled out the packaged snack and handed it to Bob's friend.

"Got a plane to catch?" the camper asked.

"Yeah, how did you know?" Bob said.

"Everybody has a plane to catch," he replied.

He slipped the straps of his pack onto his shoulders, turned and resumed walking down the trail.

"Our four o'clock plane won't wait for this mule. You

ride your mule, I'll walk let's go, we're out of here," Bob pronounced.

Bob accepted half the granola bar that was offered to him, stuffed his water bottle in his day pack and slipped his arms in the shoulder straps. The mule stood firm in the middle of the path, his head low, back and neck forming a straight, horizontal line from his tail to his ears. Suddenly his eyes rolled up and trained on Bob, who tried to look away but was caught in the mule's stare. Bob's friend mounted his mule, slipped his feet in the stirrups, gave a slight nudge with his heels and they started up the trail.

Bob stopped, looked over his shoulder and shouted, "Get everything ready. I'll be up there soon, as soon as I get this mule moving."

His friend waved and was gone. Bob walked back to the wide place on the path and sat down. Two or three small groups of hikers passed and then a couple stopped in front of Bob and asked if they could rest there.

"Whatever," Bob said.

"George and Betty Bombard from Canton. Nice to

meet you. Boy, what a fantastic place this is. I was just telling my sister Nancy. She's from Boise, wouldn't walk down with us. Yeah, she's here, right up there on top, said her legs wouldn't make it. But she's always been a complainer. Wayne, that's her husband, he said he'd go with us but felt bad about leaving Nancy all day. Of course, that's a big crock of BS. The only walking Wayne does is to the refrigerator. He never met a cheesecake he didn't like. But that's a whole different story. Janie told us not to miss this walk down to the gorge or we'd be sorry. She came here with her senior class four years ago. We didn't want to disappoint her. Say, how about a half sandwich? What was your name?"

"No thanks. It's Bob."

"Honey, give Bob half of that tuna. How long you been here, Bob?"

"Not long. Mule won't move."

"Yeah. Say, don't you have a plane to catch?"

"How did you know?"

"Everybody has a plane to catch, Bob."

"Who's Janie?" Bob asked.

"Oh, she's our daughter. Was doing great in high school, almost made the cheerleading team once, started gaining weight in sophomore year, now she's on disability from Walmart, thinking about suing them for some extra money. Kids these days, what're you going to do, Bob?"

"Walmart?"

"Well, I don't know Bob, everybody is suing them. It's the way it is in America today."

"Does she wear white tennis shoes?"

"Pretty much, when she gets out of the house, that is. She's been watching a lot of TV lately. Really likes the reality shows like that Cowboy U on Country TV. Likes to see those slickers fall off the horses and stuff like that. Likes that other one where the kids try to be pop stars by mimicking real stars. Ever see that one?"

"No, but I don't have any white tennis shoes, either," Bob said in a low voice.

The afternoon dragged on in the hot sun and the foot traffic started to dwindle. Bob zipped up his jacket and pulled the collar as high on his neck as it would go.

"Hi Bob," a twenty-something young girl greeted him as she rounded the curve in the path. "Mule still stuck?"

"How did you know about the mule…and me?"

"Down in the gorge, everybody knows," she said. "I don't think kicking him will do it, but I'd sure be tempted if it were me. Have you tried talking to him, Bob?"

Bob stared silently at her. His lips drew a tight straight line on his face. He said nothing.

"Talking can help. My boyfriend used to stop by my apartment about ten every night after drinking with his friends. He'd raid the refrigerator and then hop in the sack for a little roll in the hay. So, I told him that we needed to talk and that our relationship needed to be more multifaceted and diverse. He agreed and said we needed to go on picnics and to basketball games and to movies and he was very sympathetic and understanding. It was such a good talk and we had the best sex we ever had that night."

"Glad it worked out," Bob said.

"He never came back over, but I feel we grew as people, don't you think, Bob?"

The mule looked up and rolled his eyes. Bob nodded. After a few minutes the young girl looked studiously at Bob and spoke.

"I'm going to leave this sleeping bag for you tonight. Just drop it off with the wrangler at the top when you get that mule going."

She laid the bag down gingerly on the dusty path and resumed her upward trek. Dusk had begun to settle in and night was falling into dark.

When the morning sun shone over the South Rim of the canyon, the peaks broke the light into rainbow colors across the path where Bob laid in the sleeping bag. He rolled onto his back and smelled the flavorful aroma of bacon cooking.

"Hey there, Bob. Do you like scrambled or fried? Or I guess I could try a poached if you really want it."

"Who are you?" Bob asked.

"It's Jim. Jim is the name. Been down in the gorge camping for a few days, thought you might want a little breakfast."

"Scrambled is okay, got any toast?"

"Well, I can make toast happen. Wheat or Rye?"

"Rye is okay. Jelly?"

"All ready in a jiffy. I'm on a march this morning. Got to get to the top by nine."

"What's the rush?" Bob asked.

"Got a plane to catch. Everybody's got a...."

Bob cut him off, "I know, a plane to catch."

"I don't know what my hurry is. Pretty empty house back home. Went to court and got rid of the miserable wench last year. She had potential but I got tired of waiting for a miracle and couldn't take it anymore. She couldn't get over herself. World revolved around her, what she wanted, who she hated, who hated her, who said something that she would never forget, who used the wrong fork, who bought their clothes at the wrong store, who didn't smile just right at her pathetic parents. Screaming all the time. I tell you, Bob, sometimes it's better to cut bait and just admit that the whole thing was wrong. Life's a big experiment, don't you think?"

Bob pulled his legs up to the top of the sleeping bag,

planted his sock feet on the path and slowly stood up. His arms extended above his head in a wide stretch, and a weak groan emanated from his mouth. He rolled the sleeping bag up and inserted it into its canvas carrier, leaving no evidence he had slept on the rugged, mountain path.

"It's like a funnel, Bob. You marry this person and they have a couple of little quirks, but as time goes on, the little stuff opens up like the mouth of a funnel and, hell, this little stuff is the whole story, the whole ball of wax, the whole enchilada, and you either turn into a mouse and live with it like a caged rodent or you get the hell out, and I can tell you, my father did not raise a mouse, no; not a mouse filling these boots. You know, I like people. Sure, they can be quirky. Some can get obnoxious. You can always find something wrong with anybody. That's no fun, though."

Jim handed a plastic camping plate to Bob topped with yellow, fluffy eggs, warm bacon and toast. Bob took the plate and a paper napkin rolled around a knife, fork and spoon. Jim walked over and set a steaming cup of coffee in the sand next to Bob and lowered himself carefully onto a flat-rock seat.

"Mind if I join you?" Jim asked.

Bob nodded, barely looking up from his meal. Two hikers with large back packs passed, on their way down the trail. Almost no dust was kicked up from their boots because the damp night air deposited a thin, invisible layer of moisture on the desert soil

"Must have left the rim before dawn this morning. They'll get the best campsite," Jim opined.

A calm quiet settled in as they both concentrated on the hot breakfast before them. Then as if a small symphony took the desert stage, Mozart began seeping into Bob's ears. His right hand reached into his shirt pocket and as he pulled his cell phone out, the Mozart symphony hit a booming crescendo. Bob flipped the phone open.

"Bob here."

"I made the four o'clock plane, where are you?" Bob's friend asked.

"Eating breakfast," he replied.

"There is a two o'clock from Flagstaff. Get Al's Shuttle

Service and you won't have any trouble making it," his friend suggested. "What did you do with that stubborn mule?"

"Nothing."

"Just as well. You can't take responsibility for an animal like that," his friend said.

"Yeah," Bob said.

When Bob hung up, Jim had just finished cleaning up the breakfast gear. He stepped to the edge of the path and gazed back at the north rim. A small stretch of the river was visible but the panorama of the fourteen-mile-wide canyon dominated the spectacular view. Jim unzipped an outside pouch of his pack and extracted a small personal digital assistant. With a small stylus, he poked at the miniature screen a few times and then looked up.

"Dow's up twelve and oil dropped a dollar," he said to Bob.

He looked back at the screen and poked a little more.

"Well, plane's on time. Guess I better get a move on it," he paused. "You gotta love these little babies. Never out of touch, always on top of things, eh Bob?"

The mule's neck bent to the right and his eyes caught Bob's. Bob stared straight ahead, but didn't respond to either Jim or the mule.

"See you next time, Bob."

And Jim took off up the hill. Bob sat for a few minutes and then looked up at the mule. The mule stared straight ahead. Bob stood up, grabbed the mule's bridle and pulled as hard as he could. Then he planted his feet on the path just under the mule's nose and leaned back, applying all his weight to the effort, but the mule didn't budge.

Several groups passed on their hike up. A group of about five middle-aged adults turned at the switchback and walked toward Bob.

"You're that Bob guy, right?" one of the women said to him.

Bob looked at her but didn't respond.

"We are walking for the tsunami relief campaign in Southern California. We asked all our friends to sponsor us by giving two dollars for every mile we walk. It's a hard trail so I think two is a fair amount. Don't you, Bob?"

Bob watched her tell the story but didn't say anything.

"Tsunami relief is such a good cause. It's a massive human tragedy that could be avoided if the government were more sensitive and responsive to the needs of the people. The earthquake hit in the ocean twenty miles off the coast and the poor people in those coastal areas barely got a half-hour warning. This money is going to a good cause, a really good, important cause," she said.

Bob reached into the back pocket of his jeans and extracted his wallet. He opened it, pulled out two crisp dollar bills, and handed them to the hiker without a word. She extended her hand and accepted the money.

"Did a lot of people die?" Bob finally asked.

"Thankfully not. Actually, it was a false alarm and no tsunami materialized after the quake this time, but you never know.

"What are they going to do with the money?" Bob asked.

"Well, I haven't thought about that. Such a good cause, Bob."

The sun was rising higher in the sky and beginning to heat up the air. Bob looked out over the expanse while avoiding looking at the mule. He wanted to ask for his two dollars back before she walked away, but didn't know how to say it.

As the sun reached the midpoint in the sky, Bob sat on the flat rock and took one shoe off at a time, turned each upside-down and shook the pebbles and sand out. He re-tied the laces and then slipped the straps of his daypack onto his shoulders and picked up the sleeping bag. He walked up to the back of the mule, stopped and took a deep breath, felt like slapping the mule on the rump, but didn't. He walked up the trail about fifty yards and then stopped, turned and looked back. The mule's eyes looked straight ahead at Bob. Bob turned and started walking up the trail, which was cut into the side of the ridge and followed the contour, winding its way back and forth toward its destination on the high plateau at the rim. Bob looked over his right shoulder as the trail turned sharply up the hill. He could no longer see the mule. He took the plastic bottle from his pack and gulped the warm, clear water. The trail turned again and he suddenly stopped. Out of the corner of his eye, he caught a glimpse of the mule. He started walking again and the mule followed him, carefully keeping its distance until they reached the top. Bob walked over to the bus stop and waited. After a few minutes, a wrangler in cowboy boots with a handlebar mustache walked over and took the sleeping bag.

"Hey, I've been looking for this. Thanks Bob," he said.

The wrangler proceeded to the horse rail where the mule was standing. He unbuckled the saddle and balanced it on the tie-up rail. The bus arrived and pulled up in front of Bob, just another stop on its continuous loop of the South Rim. Bob ambled up the steps and sat down in the first row giving him a panoramic view out the front windshield. The door closed.

The driver turned toward Bob and said, "I think you'll make your 2 o'clock plane okay, Bob."

Bob looked out the side window at the pine trees surrounding the parking lot. The bus belched a burst of black diesel fumes and pulled away.

IT'S A DATE

"Do you want to talk about sex?" she said startling her lunch mate.

"Not really, not here," he said curtly, letting silence commandeer the moment.

"I just don't know why it's so important and why everybody makes such a big deal about it?" she said piercing the calm.

"Well, who said it is a big deal anyway."

"Jesus Christ, Darin, are you brain dead or did you spend the last twenty years in a cave in Siberia? I mean that is all anybody thinks about. It's all anybody talks about. Sex sells magazines. Sex sells movies. Sex sells books. Christ, sex sells sex!"

"Okay, don't get your blood pressure up. I just thought maybe there were a few other fun activities that might somehow compete with sex," he said.

"Is there any time that the engineer in you takes a rest and lets the human being, that may be lurking inside of you, talk? I mean what is the test that engineering schools use to screen students? High math scores? High cognitive skills? No imagination? No humanity, and no libido, all at the same time? Every engineer must have to pass it. Just look at the motley group of slobs we work with," she said.

"Pass the ketchup," he said cautiously.

"Did any of you guys ever hug your mother or have a dog or buy a girl a present or for Christ's sake go on a date?" she blurted out.

"My roommate at Tech had a dog once, but I didn't like him too much. None of the guys did," he said with caution mounting.

"They didn't like the roommate or the dog?" she asked.

"Oh, I guess everybody liked the dog okay," he said giving no ground.

She stared over his shoulder at the waitress walking briskly past their table. The sun trickled through the branches of an old growth live oak tree as he twitched in his chair and straightened his shoulders as if preparing for battle.

"What are you doing this weekend?" he asked.

"I thought I would find a dark room and solve some math problems, bone head!" She offered. "You know, something in the quantum physics area. Why, you wouldn't know of some atoms we could split, would you?"

"Very funny. Well, the only reason I asked is because my mother sent me a newspaper clipping about this play showing in the city. She said she saw it years ago and thought I might like it."

"What's the name of it?" she asked.

"Something about a walk in the park with George, or Gomer. Maybe it was Fred."

"You're a regular comedian. It's about George Seurat, the French painter. I studied him in Modern Art History at State," she said.

"Well, none of the guys would want to go, so maybe you would want to come along?" he said.

"Are you picking me up?"

"Yeah, that'll work. How about we go at 5:30 and stop in Chinatown for dinner before the show?" he said.

"Ok, it's a date."

BALLS ON A BRASS MONKEY… THE SEATMATE

When the day started, the sun was shining, light cumulus clouds were rolling overhead in a symphony of cotton-like clumps and the temperature was fast approaching thirty degrees. The snow was crisp but not icy and the fresh dusting of overnight powder looked to be the ideal conditions for a good day on the slopes. Bruce and Taylor could use a good day together. The past few months had strained their marriage with teenagers and money issues that seemed hard to resolve. Yet for all that had gone on, they both loved to ski and both knew the day would be a release from the mounting pressures. Taylor had grown up in New York City and as a teenager had traveled to Killington, Vermont every Saturday during the season with her ski club. Her parents were not athletic and certainly not skiers, but they liked her enthusiasm for the sport. Her father was particularly impressed with the other kids in the club and thought it was a healthy group for her to be involved with.

Bruce was a Virginian transplanted to the west coast by his career in the electronics industry. There was no opportunity to snow ski in Virginia but he had trained as a sailor and had a captain's certificate and many racing awards. He had let sailing take a back seat to raising a family and building a career but had gladly taken Taylor's prompting to learn to snow ski at Lake Tahoe.

The day was going just as planned but as lunchtime approached, the sky had become overcast and the temperature began to drop. Taylor knew that the weather could change in the mountains on a dime. Today, as was her habit, she wore an extra layer of fleece under her coat. Thirty degrees had given way to twenty and it felt like it could go to ten before the day was over.

"Do you want to go to the car and get your vest, you must be getting cold?" she asked.

"No, I'm fine. Let's just keep going. How cold could

it get anyway?" Bruce replied.

"Well, we are losing the sun and if this wind keeps picking up, we could get pretty freezing," she said. "If you change your mind, the car is not that far away."

The clouds moved in, flattening out the daylight, making it hard to see the contour of the snow, but the crispy powder allowed the skis to fly down the slopes. They were having a great time. With one more hour before the chairlifts closed, they skied right up to the entrance of a high-speed triple chair on the back side of the mountain. The chair moved slowly around the turnstile and just as they were ready to sit down, another skier appeared and plopped herself onto the empty seat next to Bruce. The chair finished its rotation and then accelerated speedily up the mountain.

"Are you cold yet, Mr. Macho?" Taylor said to Bruce.

He could barely feel the tips of his fingers and toes and the wind was cutting through his unlined jacket giving him a chill all over.

"If you really want to know, I'm colder than the balls on a brass monkey." He blurted.

Taylor lowered her mouth into her neck warmer and muffled a chuckle.

"I'm sorry but this dirty-mouth-little-boy potty humor really burns me up," said the seatmate sitting next to Bruce. "We try all our lives to create clean surroundings and a healthy environment and all a person hears is this gross 'stuff'," she said. "I suppose next you will say, 'stay pretty die young', or the check's in the mail'. Can't you moronic men get half a clue that life is not about smart-ass sayings and slamming other people. Look, if there were better ways to say the things that you are thinking, I mean, more straight forward and sensitive, wouldn't you feel better about yourself? I can tell you right here, to your face, that people would feel better about you."

Taylor quietly turned her head and pulled the neck warmer up over her nose, covering as much of her face as she could.

"If men would honestly express themselves and cut out the digs and the innuendos maybe the world would be a better place. Maybe we could clean up the oceans, or have more hybrid cars, or finally defund the police. Do you know what I mean?" the seatmate continued.

Just then Bruce's eyes focused in on relief as the chairlift was unloading just six feet away. He reached over with his right hand and took one of the ski poles from the pair and as the chair slowed, he lifted off the seat and propelled himself first forward and then turned to the left. He didn't stop to adjust his pole straps but went straight for the first crest about three hundred yards down the mountain. Taylor skied in like a rocket ship behind him. Drawing her skis together, turning her hips and shoulders uphill, the left edges of her skis dug into the powdery snow and she stopped on a dime next to Bruce.

"I liked her sense of humor, didn't you?" she asked.

"Right. Forget skiing, it's time for a drink," he replied.

Twenty minutes later Bruce and Taylor were sitting in front of a fire at the lodge. His feet and hands were warming up. The waitress set down a bottle of Sierra Nevada Pale Ale and a shot glass full of fine Tennessee whiskey in front of Bruce. Taylor lifted her glass of white wine in the air and offered a toast to bizarre events. He lifted the whiskey glass and without a word emptied the contents.

"Hello again," said a voice from behind their chairs. "I thought I recognized you two by your matching hats. I know we didn't finish our conversation on the lift. Mind if I join you?" said the seatmate.

Bruce made a quick glance toward Taylor and then addressed the woman. "Before you get started, I want to tell you that I was raised as a sailor. I captained sloops, schooners, and catamarans all over the Caribbean by the time I was twenty-five. There is a rich sailing history in trade, warfare, and even technology. Did you know that during the development of steam engines, there was a time when hybrid ships were powered with both sails and steam?"

The seatmate started to shift back and forth on her feet and began to look anxious. She looked over at Taylor but got no help. Taylor was relaxing in her overstuffed lounge chair sipping her wine. She didn't know where Bruce was going with this but she loved to listen to him reel out his stories. He always made them up as he went, but they always ended with an interesting twist. She had heard other Southerners tell stories, but Bruce was the best.

"Well, I didn't know that," said the seatmate. "But back to…"

Bruce non-apologetically cut her off and resumed his tale. "Anyway, warfare technology has come a long way since the days of sailing ships."

"That's what I am talking about, boys and their war toys. Come on, do we really need all this conflict. In the end, don't people all want the same things in life," the seatmate interjected.

"Like flying airplanes into tall buildings," Taylor said jumping into the fray.

Bruce jerked his head around and looked straight at Taylor. His lips were pursed and his eyes drilled into hers displaying a tacit disapproval. Then his head dropped to the left and he hung his tongue out the left side of his mouth as if he were hanging in an imaginary noose. Taylor closed her mouth tightly trying to hold back the giggle that was spontaneous and inevitable. He was an incorrigible cutup. The seatmate was gathering her thoughts and missed the couple's exchange.

"Well during those days, the merchant ships carried

goods and passengers around the world and their first and best defense when being attacked was to out run the attacker. But if they had to fight, they almost always had a few canons on board to protect the helpless women and children passengers and to protect the raw goods that were used in factories to provide jobs for poor working people which provided opportunities to put milk on the table for their hungry babies."

Taylor looked down at the wine glass in her hand and pressed her lips together to keep from laughing out loud. Bruce was pushing the limits of schmaltz and she wondered if he was going to burst into a comedy routine. She looked up for the waitress. She was going to need more wine.

Bruce saw her but continued. "The pirates had many rows of guns and it was rare that a merchant ship could survive a direct attack. But one thing all the ships had in common was a large rack that was in the hold of the ship that held the cannon balls. This rack was originally made of brass and was referred to as the brass monkey. Now sometimes during winter the lower decks of the ships would get very cold and the cannon balls would almost be too cold to touch and so sometimes when the sailors felt really cold and were missing their mommies, they would express their feelings to their friends and say 'they were colder than the balls on a brass monkey'. It was insensitive, but you know how men are."

Taylor brought her glass to her lips and drained the last swallow of the wine into her mouth when Bruce said, "Now if you will excuse me, I have to see a man about a horse."

Taylor clamped her mouth closed and tried to stop the gush of air up through her throat, but it was futile. The rush of air broke through her mouth and took the wine with it and right into the flabbergasted face of the seatmate.

When Bruce returned, a fresh glass of whiskey was on the table and no seatmate was in sight.

"How did you get rid of her?" Bruce asked.

"I told her I would break both of her legs if she didn't leave us alone."

"You didn't either," he said.

"Well not exactly, but I did get rid of her. Let's have a toast." She raised her fresh glass of wine and said, "Here's to the seatmate…and the brass monkey."

THE BLAST

Abdul gazed across the room through the window past the fountain and landscaped grounds to the endless sea of burning sand. His two-day-old beard had not yet started to itch as he knew it soon would. The talk around the table of oil prices and drilling problems drifted into his ears and out again. Although he was Deputy Minister of Finance and controlled the budgets for trillions of dollars, he had no interest in the wimpy dribblings of capitalism.

He had reached his mid-forties as a thriving member of the royal family, had a PhD in finance from Stanford University, a wife and six children and, as deputy finance minister, the second highest job in finance in the Kingdom. While his promotion to the top slot was assured, he had from years past, an emptiness, and a profound feeling of uncertainty down in his soul.

Searching out dissident groups had been easier than he

had thought. The Royal family was so vast and wealthy that too much leisure time, adolescent angst and distrust had fueled the flames of deceit for him. By the time Abdul ascended to the position of Deputy Minister, he was fully involved and living a secret, dual existence as a leader of the most radical, anti-western group in the country.

Abdul glanced around the large oval conference table, slowly turned with a thoughtful, nonchalant air and moved to the back of the room. He extended his right hand and grasped the polished brass doorknob, turning it slightly and pulling the door toward him. As the door opened, he quietly slipped through it and into the hallway. His gaze stayed low as he moved quickly to the third door on the right and vanished into his private study. His five-foot ten-inch frame sunk into the sumptuous velour upholstery of his desk chair. The fragrance of fresh cut roses filled his nose and the wide panorama of immaculately manicured grounds stared at him through the large picture window. He lowered his chin comfortably and closed his eyes.

At that moment, in another country, the sun was

beating down in a scorching blaze on a single-story concrete house. The temperature had reached 100 degrees inside as the antiquated ventilation system strained to keep up with the desert heat. When Abdul opened his eyes, the sun nearly blinded him, pouring in through the bare window. He rose from the brown metal folding chair and walked through the cluttered, dark hallway into a meeting room where eleven men stood around a map table. The discussion was exclusively about strategy and timing because the target had already been chosen. The Inter-Continental Hotel in Jakarta would be bombed next month during the height of the Israeli holiday season. Only the finishing touches needed to be ironed out. The young man leading the discussion looked up as Abdul entered the room.

"Glad you are back, leader. How long can you stay?"

Abdul paused before speaking. The others stayed focused on the map and no one looked up.

"I cannot stay long but I wanted you to know that the money has been transferred and is safe in our French bank. The passports and visas have been arranged. The attack will be completed, praise Allah." Abdul said with quiet resolve.

Each man seemed to understand yet no one moved and no one uttered a reply.

He turned and walked through the hall, sidestepping a stack of old, useless computer parts. Entering the drab monotone room from which he had emerged, he stopped and took a deep breath. The paint was peeling away under the window sill all the way to the floor. As he sat in the dilapidated chair, he lowered his chin and closed his eyes. When his eyes opened, he looked out the picture window to the water fountain and manicured grass that surrounded the palace. The window sill was finished in gilded gold leaf and the walls were covered in a rich burgundy fabric from Spain. He didn't worry about being missed in the meeting because only eleven minutes had elapsed. The other ministers talked endlessly about oil issues; the problems were always the same and the solutions were always the same.

The rebel group never questioned his sudden appearances and disappearances. Although many in the leadership had formal education, the folklore and tradition in their culture was rife with stories and legends of magic and the supernatural. Abdul had relegated these legends himself, to superstition and childish gibberish with no basis in reality during his early life. During his years in graduate school at Stanford University, the 1970's in Northern California was a hotbed of new wave experimentation. He had inadvertently wondered into the Palo Alto Psychic Institute one Saturday afternoon and paid $25 for an aura reading. He found it fascinating. After attending classes for a year, he became interested in one of the most fantastic areas in the psychic realm, telekinesis or the art of moving objects with the mind. Nobody at the school knew much about it but most of the experienced teachers were confident it could be done. Abdul became very adept at bending spoons with his mind but he wanted to move larger objects in real time. One day, as he sat alone at the school contemplating the problem, he slowly dropped his chin and closed his eyes. When he opened his eyes, he was in his living room at his apartment on Alma Street. He was shocked and disoriented but maintained his composure long enough to notice that no time had elapsed while he had physically moved about two miles. He decided to tell no one about this event. Over the next year he perfected the technique and could select the location and timing of his move. He found that no distance was too far and any location was achievable. He never shared the knowledge of his power with anyone nor did he know of anyone else who had his capability.

#

As the February morning sun rose and light filled Abdul's bedroom, he awoke and rang the small bell that had lain quietly on his bed stand throughout the night. Within ten-minutes his breakfast of strawberry yogurt, buttered toast and orange juice was set on his table. He sat quietly eating the yogurt and then the toast. In less than half an hour, dressed in a black custom-made suit and soft leather shoes from Italy, he holstered a .57 magnum automatic pistol under his coat. Sitting in his chair he lowered his chin. When he opened his eyes, he was alone in room 3720 at the Inter-continental Hotel in Jakarta. He walked out the door and took the elevator to the lobby where he found a plush emerald green chair facing the wall of glass that greeted visitors to the front entrance. He watched his comrade enter the front door and place the large trunk on its side at the bell captain's station. Their eyes met for a brief second as the accomplice turned to leave.

The device was set up to trigger the explosion ten-seconds after it was tripped. The process was surprisingly simple. The remote control that Abdul now held in his right hand would transmit a signal to the detonator inside the trunk, causing a bead of mercury to be released through a set of chambers which, when reaching two electrodes in the final chamber, completed the circuit and detonated the bomb. The trunk needed to be standing on its side vertically in order for the mercury to be pulled down by gravity, otherwise the ten-second delay would be reduced to a no-second delay.

Everything had been accomplished perfectly. Abdul was proud of his team. They had entered the city undetected, acquired the necessary explosives and would be nowhere near the scene when the explosion occurred.

He took another look at the scurrying tourist and hotel staff buzzing in and out of the lobby. The fingers of his right hand tightened around the remote control and his thumb found the red button, as he eyed the trunk. He depressed the red button and began to move his chin down. As his eyes began to shut, he saw the bell captain pick up the trunk and lay it horizontally on the floor to make room for additional luggage. The mercury quickly bypassed the interim chambers and engulfed the electrodes, completing the circuit. The blast ripped through the lobby and the mezzanine and blew a forty-foot gap in the floor above the underground parking garage. Of the 170 known dead, 101 were Jakartan, 62 Israeli, 6 British and one Deputy Minister of Finance.

Two More Pieces of Pie

Jolene skipped out of the front door letting the screen door slam behind her. No doubt another sliver or two of brown paint pealed away from the door frame and settled onto the outdoor porch unnoticed. As she slid into the driver's seat of the two-tone 1973 Ford Ranger, she allowed her mind to examine just why she felt carefree and happy when everything in her life was not necessarily on track. "I guess there really is an actual track somewhere," she thought.

After her 14th birthday she had started waitressing in her grandfather's barbeque restaurant in the foothills of southern California between the coast and the central valley. Now three years later and about to finish high school, Jolene worked the busy weekend schedule, drove the hand-me-down truck and felt like she should be doing more with her life going forward, but unsure what that might look like.

School had worked out okay and her grades were above average. She even took all the math and science courses that were recommended for the college prep track. Not that she liked either discipline, she just wanted to prove she could do it. But Jolene liked music and she was a natural talent at just about any instrument she picked up. The high school had hired an extremely talented music teacher three years before Jolene's freshman year. Mr. Johns had completed a master's degree from the Julliard School and was playing in both the Baltimore and Philadelphia symphony orchestras. One day after visiting Los Angeles, he rented a car and drove up the coast for the day. As he wound along the shoestring ribbon of Highway 1 heading north from Santa Barbara, he turned right, onto a nondescript paved road winding into the coastal hills. After fifteen miles, he pulled into the dusty gravel parking lot of the Bob-a-Que Family Restaurant. It was nearly six in the evening, and Mr. Johns sat alone, looking out his window at an endless expanse of live oak trees and the accompanying clutter that littered the hills with nature's debris at the base of each rugged trunk. Over his right shoulder he turned to see thirty-five acres of vineyards in straight rows bathed in the pastel light of a California setting sun.

Mr. Johns made a decision at that moment of epiphany. His transition was swift, shocking his friends and family, but leveling a sharper blow to the symphony itself. When Mr. Johns began his first class in the band room of Paso Robles high school, it had barely been six months, but the harvest was beginning for the season and he could hardly wait to watch the grape crush on Saturday and Sunday. He rarely ever thought of his previous life as a top symphony violinist. His decision was quick but also final. After the crush activity wound down Saturday, he planned to stop by the Bob-a-Que for the catfish dinner fresh from the coast that afternoon.

Jolene clearly played Vivaldi the best, and it was no wonder, because he was her favorite of all the classical composers. The fingers of her left hand stroked the violin strings of her school issued instrument into a purring complacency like a mother cajoling her baby to sleep. Mr. Johns had literally put the violin in Jolene's hands and showed her how to hold it and how to move the bow. To his amazement, he needed to show Jolene very little else about the instrument and the music itself came to her just as easily. But she only spent the required school time on classical music and saved the passion for the roadhouse jams.

On Friday and Saturday nights the house band played until nine o'clock. After that, often a jam would begin for an hour until closing time, that is unless Jolene's grandfather jumped in on the congas or piano, which could easily extent the fun 'til midnight. Jolene liked to sit in with the house band on piano in between serving up the ribeye or the porterhouse steaks. If the cook saw her mount the stage, he would slow up the orders a little giving the rest of the patrons a little more musical time. Jolene first started playing the bass with the band in the days when she had to stand on a chair to reach the top of the neck. She never had a lesson, but a few years of quiet watching was all she needed. She could slap out those bass runs just like a pro.

Mr. Johns had told Jolene about the East Coast classical

music scene. Although a somewhat unconventional applicant he was quite confident he could get her accepted at the Berkeley School of Music in Boston or maybe even Julliard itself. She was ambitious after all and why not follow an ambition at her age? She admired Mr. Johns even though she was a little befuddled about his colossal career change. But she knew the hills, the vineyards and the Pacific Ocean she loved, would always be here for her to come home to. In fact, the excitement of a big move and an exciting career had driven her to complete applications to the Berkeley School, Julliard and Carnegie Mellon as a back up school. The finishing touches were just now completed and the mailing deadline was fast approaching.

When Mr. Johns walked in the Bob-a-Que Restaurant, Jolene was just starting a fiddle solo with the house band. They normally stuck to country music or some jazz inspired country songs known as western swing. But this one was a bluegrass song made famous by the Virginia bluegrass king, Bill Monroe, called "Uncle Pen". There was plenty of room for instrumental solos originally played by Monroe on the mandolin, but nobody was missing the shrill staccato of the mandolin when Jolene's fingers flew over the strings in a soft delicate but determined movement. The short notes pounded like a six-pound hammer on a nail and the long notes hung in the air like an angel in church. After her solo, the lead singer weaved his high tenor voice into the second verse and Jolene unceremoniously ducked off stage and headed for the kitchen. She had a table of six with three catfish dinners, and two split orders of the giant porterhouse steak to deliver. As she set the last dinner in front of the customer, she leaned over and whispered, "Only two more pieces of pie left. You better order them now."

Mr. Johns was looking forward to an early evening and slipped out after dinner. Jolene finished her last table, gathered up the tips and left before closing. Nobody really missed her. The clean up was routine and she had had a long night. On the way home she pulled into the small country store about two miles from the restaurant. It was a sleepy little store all the time but tonight it was nearly dead asleep. She bought a pack of sugarless gum, got back in the truck and pulled out of the parking lot. Just before the driveway joined the road, she stopped next to a phone booth. Reaching next to her on the front bench seat, she grabbed the three envelopes containing her school applications. Sliding out the driver's seat, she walked over toward the phone booth. As her steps shortened and she drew to a stop, she looked over her shoulder at the dilapidated store front she had just left and then gazed up at the sky and was not surprised to see the Big Dipper now directly overhead. Jolene looked down at the rusted steel barrel beside her. It had been used as a trash and debris can for just the amount of time it takes to nearly rot one side out completely. She gave a quick glance at the can's position, looked out again at the wide open sky, took a deep breath, then tossed the envelops in. They hit the back side and settled in on top of the well seasoned contents of mostly cans and bottles. She got back in the truck and headed home. "Not much to do tomorrow," she thought, "guess I'll sleep late."

ABOUT THE AUTHOR

Rick Glaze published *The Purple River in 2021*, *Spanish Pieces of Eight* in 2022, *Ralph & Murray* in 2023, and *Eight Pieces of Eight in 2025*. Rick was a financial columnist in Silicon Valley for San Francisco's *Nob Hill Gazette* and the *Los Altos Town Crier*. He attended the Stanford University Creative Writing Program, and is a graduate of Peabody College, Vanderbilt University. An award-winning songwriter, with a Pandora radio station, credits on Country Music Television (CMT), and BBC Radio, Rick has rafted the Grand Canyon, the Salmon and Rogue Rivers as well as sailed throughout the Caribbean Sea.

Go to RickGlaze.com for updates on the Islands,
Treasure Hunts, videos, and new stories.

www.ingramcontent.com/pod-product-compliance
Lightning Source LLC
Chambersburg PA
CBHW051235210726
48290CB00003B/979
* 9 7 8 1 7 3 7 2 9 5 1 9 8 *